M000222474

THE SECRET OF
LOCKER 24

Wil Mara

An imprint of Enslow Publishing

WEST **44** BOOKS™

THE SECRET OF LOCKER 24	HOUSE OF A MILLION ROOMS
A POOL OF DEATHLY BLUE	THE TIME TRAP
THE OTHER	WHERE DID MY FAMILY GO?!
THE VIDEOMANIAC	THE GIRL WHO GREW NASTY THINGS

Please visit our website, www.west44books.com. For a free color catalog of all our high-quality books, call toll free 1-800-398-2504.

Cataloging-in-Publication Data
Names: Mara, Wil.
Title: The secret of locker 24 / Wil Mara.
Description: New York : West 44, 2023. | Series: Twisted
Identifiers: ISBN 9781978596221 (pbk.) | ISBN 9781978596214 (library bound) | ISBN 9781978596238 (ebook)
Subjects: LCSH: Bullying--Juvenile fiction. | Bullying in schools--Juvenile fiction. | School--Juvenile fiction.
Classification: LCC PZ7.M373 Se 2023 | DDC [F]--dc23

Published in 2023 by
Enslow Publishing LLC
101 West 23rd Street, Suite #240
New York, NY 10011

Designer: Rachel Rising

Photo Credits: Cover, Everyonephoto Studio/Shutterstock.com; Cover, C2matic Photography/Shutterstock.com; Cover, faestock/Shuttestock.com; pp. 6, 27, 38, 45, 52, 60, 64 gaga.vastard/Shutterstock.com.

Printed in the United States of America

CPSIA compliance information: Batch #CS23W44: For further information contact Enslow Publishing LLC, New York, New York at 1-800-398-2504.

TWISTED

For Eileen, who wanted to know

"Maybe we should just get pizza," Emily said as she strode briskly down the school's central hallway. A well-worn backpack hung from her shoulder. The morning sunlight through the high windows drew bright rectangles on the polished floor. "We haven't done pizza in forever."

"That's a good idea," her mom replied through the little Bluetooth device in Emily's ear. It looked like a black bug trying to burrow into her head. "I could stop at King's on the way home from work."

"Yes! King's has the best Sicilian!"

"And your father likes their garlic knots."

"Perfect."

"Will you place the order?" her mom asked. "Say, around five thirty?"

Emily turned the corner into another hallway. This one was lined on either side with hundreds of lockers. "If I'm home I will."

"You don't think you'll be home by five thirty?!"

"I'm going to try my best."

"Em, you've been working yourself to death lately. And if a parent is saying that to their middle schooler, then it must be true."

Emily smiled. "I know. It's been busy. But we're getting close to the end of the year. That means the *yearbook* has to get done really soon. And since I'm in charge of it …"

"Yeah, yeah, I know. You've told me a million times. You have to send it to the printer by some deadline."

Emily arrived at her locker and started

spinning the dial. "Next Tuesday. And it can't be late. It's *already* late, actually." She got the lock open on the first try and removed it. The door swung back with a familiar squeal. "If we don't get the files sent to the printing company by then, we're in big trouble. This is a great school, and it deserves to have a great yearbook. A *perfect* yearbook, in fact, because that's what this school *really* is."

"No school is perfect, Em. I know you've always thought that, but—"

"Ours is."

Her mom let out a long sigh. "Okay, whatever. Y'know, when I was a kid, we didn't have—"

"Electricity?"

"Funny. No, we didn't have packed schedules like you do. We had maybe one extracurricular activity after school. Not four or five like you guys do. And you're only in eighth grade!"

"It's fine," Emily said. "Truly."

Half the backpack's contents went into the locker. Then a roughly equal amount came out. One of those items was a T-shirt that said Haddenport Hornets on the front.

"You're all going to have heart attacks before you're thirty," her mom added.

Emily rolled her eyes. "If Josh, Hailey, and Chloe don't get their yearbook stuff to me soon, I'm going to have a heart attack long before then. Those three are basically holding everything up. Especially Hailey."

She closed the door and set the lock back in place. Then she gave it a quick tug.

"Mom, I gotta go," she said.

"Running?"

"Yeah, I want to do a few laps around the track before we start practice. Then I gotta get to my first class."

Her mom chuckled. "Unbelievable. Okay, I'll talk to you in a little while. Love you, sweetie."

"Love you too. Bye."

Emily pressed and held the button on the Bluetooth to disconnect it from her phone. She knew that Bluetooth earpieces weren't considered particularly cool or fashionable by her classmates. But they were just so *efficient.* That hands-free thing allowed her to do all sorts of stuff while she was talking to somebody. *Try doing anything while you've got the phone trapped between your head and your shoulder,* she had thought many times. *Good luck with that.*

She put the earpiece into the same pocket as her phone. Then she slung the backpack over her shoulder and started walking in the direction of the athletic fields.

Just a few steps later, however, she stopped

again. And what she saw was one of those things that's hard to believe even when you're looking right at it. In fact, it was basically impossible.

No, a voice in her mind said quietly.

It can't be …

Emily stood there for a time, glued in place. Her eyes shifted left and right to survey the hall. There was no one else around. Not even the sound of anyone nearby.

She took a cautious step forward. Then another. Now she was close enough to touch it.

Locker 24. THE Locker 24 …

It was open maybe an inch. Barely enough to slip your hand in sideways. Not that she had any intention of doing that. *Not a chance*, she thought. *Not one chance in a zillion.*

It looked like every other locker in the school. It was painted the same red color. Had the same vent lines at the top. The same chrome hardware. And hanging from the handle, now opened and dangling, was the same type of lock everyone else used. The kind with the black number dial.

Except this locker isn't like the others, that mind-voice reminded her. *Not even close. So what's going on here?*

She had no idea. Locker 24 wasn't supposed to be opened. Not by her or anyone else. Ever. *Was it already open when I got here?* she wondered. She felt like she would've noticed that. Then again, she was on the phone with her mom, so maybe she just didn't see it.

The urge to open it a little further and

look inside was becoming more powerful by the second. She knew she shouldn't. It was definitely not The Right Thing to Do, and Emily always did The Right Thing. She was, in fact, very proud of herself for that. Not because it made all the grown-ups happy or kept her out of trouble. It just seemed to make sense to live that way. It was much easier. And much more *efficient.*

Except for right now.

There was no sense denying it. Emily was very curious about what was in there. This was her last year at Haddenport Middle School, and she had wondered what was inside this locker many times. Now it seemed as though her curiosity could finally be satisfied. *If only that door was opened just a few more inches …*

She reached for it, her finger sticking out. The moment it connected with the cold metal, however, she pulled it back.

"No," she said out loud. "No, no, no."

She closed the door and snapped the lock shut, giving the dial a final spin for good measure.

Good, she told herself. *That's the end of that.* She didn't know who had opened it in the first place, and she didn't care. If they were that determined, they'd come back and do it again. It didn't look *forced* open, she noticed. The lock was in perfect working order. *And who would even know the combination after all these years?* She hadn't a clue, but then she didn't have the time to puzzle out such details. She had a million other things going on. She had to get moving. And as for the urge to find out what was in there—

Well, it'll just have to stay an urge, she told herself.

She turned and hurried down the hallway.

Emily sat at the desk in her room later that night trying to concentrate. But she just couldn't.

She'd already finished her math and history homework. She usually loved history, but tonight she had to drag herself through it. And now she was onto the yearbook stuff again. There was so much left to do. Being in charge of the yearbook sounded like fun back in September. But now it seemed like a ridiculous idea. Making a book was like doing a jigsaw puzzle, except you didn't just fit the pieces together. You had to create them all, too. And if she had any hope of success, she really had to *concentrate*. That had never been a problem for her before. So why was it so tough now?

That little voice in her head spoke out

again—*Because of the locker …*

Emily sat back in her chair and crossed her arms.

"Yeah," she said. "That's what it is."

She hadn't given it too much thought during the day because she'd been so busy. And after she got home, she was hanging with her family and eating another killer Sicilian pizza. It wasn't until she came up here that she started thinking about it again.

I'll call Bryce. He'll know more.

She smiled. Bryce Wilson was one of the funniest, most daring people she'd ever met. He was a sophomore at Haddenport High now. But two years ago he was the editor-in-chief for the *Haddenport Bugle*, the middle school's newspaper. He made an unforgettable impression right from the first day. Emily had only been at the school for a few weeks and had never worked on a school paper before. But she wanted to give it a try. No sooner had she walked through the door than Bryce was staring at her with his hands on his hips. He asked if she was interested in "shaking things up." As it turned out, that was his whole outlook on life. Shake people up, make them uncomfortable, and force them to look at the world a little differently. He also, amazingly, managed to do this in a way that still made him entirely likable. He was pushy, yes. But he was also positive, and she really admired that.

Most people her age would text or direct message someone. But Emily didn't have time for that. She liked to be even more direct—so she called. Bryce answered her call by saying, "No way." Emily could tell he was smiling.

"Way," she said back. "How are you doing, Bryce?"

"How I'm doing is just fine, Ems. Just very

fine and good and great and awesome."

"Causing more trouble, I'm guessing?"

"Better believe it. I got kicked off the high school paper five times since I've been here. *Five times!* And yet, they keep bringing me back. Popular demand, y'know? My readers can't get enough of me!"

Emily laughed. "I have no trouble believing that."

"What about you? What's happening in Emilyville? You still keeping out of trouble?"

"Trying my best," she said.

"I'm sure you are. Never wanted to cause any waves like I do."

"Well …" She paused, trying to figure out how much she should say. "Maybe that's not completely true at the moment."

"*Whaaaaat?* Are my ears deceiving me? Wait, how long have I been asleep?!"

"Bryce, no kidding. I have a question about something."

"You ask, and I shall answer," he said boldly. "Fire away."

"Okay. It's about Locker 24."

There was nothing but silence from the other end. And it lasted so long that Emily thought maybe the signal had dropped.

"Hey, are you still th—"

"You're not serious," he said finally. And it wasn't in his Bryce tone, either. With this one question, Emily had knocked all the Bryce-ness right out of him.

"Of course, I'm serious. Why wouldn't I b—"

"You don't want to go messing with that, kiddo," he told her. "No sir, uh-uh."

"No? Why not?"

"Are you thinking about writing another

article about it? Like I tried to do?"

"I'm not on the paper this year. I've got too much else going on. But yeah, I know *you* tried to write one. Then, all of a sudden, you stopped. So I was wondering what happened with that."

There was another long pause, which Emily found utterly fascinating. She'd never known Bryce to be short on something to say.

"What happened was I got into trouble," he told her in the same flatline tone. "*Big* trouble."

"So what? You were always getting into trouble for stuff you—"

"Not like this. Ems, I'm telling you, something's seriously wrong there. Seriously wrong."

"Like what?"

"Like I don't know. Like I couldn't find out. From anyone. No one would talk about it. Not Mr. Hart, not Mrs. Goldsmith, not even Mr.

Hadermeyer. Since when does Mr. Hadermeyer refuse to spill about something?"

Bryce was right—Mr. Hadermeyer was always happy to talk to the kids. He'd been the head custodian forever. And he knew *everything* about the school there was to know. He was old and crabby and nice and funny, all at the same time. And there was nothing he loved more than telling stories.

"From the day I started at the school, I heard people talking about that locker," Bryce went on. "And they were all saying the same thing— *don't*. Don't look at it, don't touch it. And the biggest don't of all, don't ask about it. The subject was *closed*, you know what I mean? I couldn't even find out the name of the last person who used it."

"That's incredible."

"Finally, I was marched into the principal's office. Mr. Ellis told me not to make any more inquiries for my article. That's exactly what he said. 'Son, you will not make any more inquiries into that locker.' He called me son. And he didn't even say 'Locker 24.' He just said *the* locker, like everyone would know which one he meant."

"Which, I guess, everyone would."

"Exactly. He said I'd get detention if I didn't stop, and suspension after that. I thought he was just blowing smoke, y'know, to scare me. But when I got home, my parents were pretty upset, too."

Emily's eyes widened. "He called your *parents?*"

"He sure did. And my father told me if I didn't do what Mr. Ellis said … well, let's just say I got the message loud and clear. And that's when I dropped the story. The one and only time I ever did that."

"Wow …"

"Why are you interested in all this, anyway?"

Emily found herself struggling again to figure out how much she should reveal. If Bryce knew the locker had been opened, he'd jump on the story again. The fact that he was no longer at the middle school wouldn't make any difference. She could tell he was still angry about being forced to stop last time. Then again, he might get into even more trouble than before. *And I don't want that,* she thought. *He's completely nuts, but in a good way. A really good way.* She didn't want to see anything happen to him.

"I heard some kids talking about it today," she told him. "And it just got me thinking."

"Well, you should think about something else instead," he said. "That locker is bad news. *Very* bad news. If a troublemaker like me can't mess with it, then a nice, rule-abiding person like you shouldn't, either."

She smiled and realized he was right.

Why was she even bothering with something so unimportant? She had tons to do every day. Schoolwork, homework, running, extracurricular stuff.

The yearbook …

Ugh, yeah … the yearbook. That alone was going to require so much energy and focus. She really didn't have time to play detective. Besides, she closed the locker as soon as she saw that it was open. And she put the lock back in place, too. So that was the end of it, right?

Yes, that's the end of it.

This is what Emily Turner told herself.

When Emily got to the main hallway early the next morning, she couldn't believe her luck. Josh was at the other end with a bunch of his friends from the lacrosse team, Max Gad and Brady Clarke. They must have had a super-early practice. *One of the three people I need to see …*

"Hey!" she yelled, breaking into a jog. She passed Locker 24 and gave it only a quick glance. The door was shut and the lock in place, just as she'd left it yesterday.

Josh was tall and lanky with a mess of curly brown hair. He and his friends were part of what Emily thought of as the "rich club." Their parents had serious money, so they all *looked* like they had serious money. Emily knew some of the other kids in the school couldn't stand them, but she didn't have any problems. They always treated her fine. And Josh was a legacy kid on the yearbook staff. His grandfather had worked on the yearbook, his father had worked on the yearbook ... and now he did. He had a place on the staff before Emily even started choosing the staff.

Josh smiled when he saw her.

"Hey!" he said back with a wave. "What's up, Turner?"

"We're getting close to the deadline for the yearbook," she said when she reached him. "We really need your stuff."

The stuff in question was all the sports content. Pictures from practices and games, plus captions. Josh had been excited about it from the start. And he knew how to take really good pictures. What he *didn't* seem to understand was the concept of a schedule.

He nodded. "Right, my stuff. Well, it's almost ready. I've got all the pics, I just need to write all the captions."

"When do you think that'll be done?"

He shrugged. "Next week sometime?"

Emily felt impatient. Through tight lips, she asked, "Can you get it all to me by next *Monday*?"

"If I work on it over the weekend, sure."

Emily grinned. "*Are* you going to work on it over the weekend?"

Josh's friends started laughing. One of them poked him and said, "Ohhh, she's going to get you if you don't do your *work*, Josh!"

Josh pushed his friend half-heartedly and told him to shut it. Then, back to Emily, he said, "Yeah, Monday's cool."

"Excellent, thanks."

She turned and started to her own locker.

That was one thing done. She checked it off her long mental to-do list.

Just before she got to her locker, she noticed Hailey at the other end of the hallway. Hailey wore thick glasses that were shaped like cat's eyes. Her blond hair had purple streaks in it. Her shoes were covered in Sharpie doodles.

She was standing there, staring in Emily's direction.

"Hey!" Emily said with a wave. "Can I talk to you for a sec—"

But Hailey looked past Emily. Her eyes widened. Then she turned and walked away.

"Hailey! Hey!"

When she got to the end of the hall and looked around the corner, Hailey was nowhere to be seen.

"Wow, I guess she doesn't want to talk to me," Emily grumbled before going back to her locker.

Like the day before, it was a matter of putting a bunch of things in and taking a bunch of things out. She had a math test that mattered and a history test that really didn't. But she had studied equally hard for both because that's what straight-A students did.

Then she remembered something else she needed to tell Josh. He had to take a few more basketball pictures because there didn't seem to be enough of those. But when she looked, he and his crew were already gone. Then she looked the other way and found that she was now in the hallway by herself.

I'll text him, she thought as she closed her locker and pulled her phone out.

She started walking as she typed the message. Then she came to a dead stop again, her eyes wide with disbelief.

"No way …" she whispered.

Locker 24 was open a little more than last time. It had been maybe an inch yesterday. Now it was two or three inches. Enough to put your hand in without having to turn it. *And more than enough to take a peek inside*, she realized.

She could see a few things in there already. The details were lost in the shadows. But she could make out shapes. They would become clearer if she got some light in there. Light from, say, her phone.

She stood there for a moment trying to decide what to do. One part of her wanted to close it, lock it, and forget about it again. But another part realized something that should've been obvious to her already.

The locker WANTS you to open it. It WANTS you to see what's inside.

Emily had always considered herself a

reasonable person. Not someone given to what her grandma called "wild flights of fancy." The very idea that the locker wanted her to see inside was ridiculous. As if it was some living, breathing thing.

Then how come I'm not laughing? she wondered. *How come I'm not rolling my eyes at such a stupid idea?*

Because the cold truth was that the locker had opened *itself*. There was no one else around who could've done it. And, she realized, it had happened two days in a row. Both times o*nly when she was here by herself.* No one else—just her. Also, this time it opened a little more than before. As if it was insisting that she look. *You keep ignoring me, I'll just keep opening.* That's what it seemed to be saying.

She checked every which way to make sure there wasn't anyone who could see her. But there wasn't—the coast was clear.

She set her fingers on the door just above the lock. Then she pulled it open all the way.

It was all the normal stuff you'd expect to find in an eighth-grader's locker. A well-worn backpack sitting on the bottom. A jacket hanging on the hook. A few textbooks on the top shelf. And some spiralbound notebooks on top of those. There were stickers on the inside of the door, too. A unicorn beneath an explosive rainbow. A heart with the word LOVE across the middle. And a hand curled into the thumbs-up position. There were also a few logos of '90s bands that her parents liked. Nirvana, Green Day, Soundgarden, Rage Against the Machine.

So what's the big deal? This is what all the fuss is about?

No, she decided, there had to be more. She had to dig deeper if she wanted to get to the bottom of this. Another of her grandma's favorite sayings was "The devil's in the details." That meant the truth behind any mystery lay in the little things. And she certainly wasn't going to find any of those by standing here and staring.

She took out the jacket. Dark blue, very thin. A windbreaker. She put her hand in each of the pockets. There was a gum wrapper, a dime, three pennies, and an old pen.

She returned that to its hook and took out the backpack. There was another textbook inside, and a paperback novel titled *To Kill a Mockingbird.* That would be on the required reading list in high school, Emily knew. In the backpack's front pocket, there were two more pens and a pencil.

She returned the backpack and took down one of the spiral notebooks. The cover was made of very thin cardboard. Along the top, there was a name written in black ink—*Sage Kimenski.* Under the name was a date—*September 2002.*

Emily had never heard of her. Not that she expected to, since Kimenski had been a student here more than two decades ago. The handwriting was in script, and it was absolutely beautiful. Every letter seemed to have its own special character. Yet they all fit together to form what seemed like a single piece of art. Kimenski's penmanship was so perfect, in fact, that it almost looked fake.

Emily opened the notebook to a random page. There weren't any mathematical equations or notes on a battle from the Civil War. Instead she found more artwork. *Real* artwork. And it was some of the most incredible art she had ever seen.

Whoever Sage Kimenski was, her talent was off the charts. On one page, she'd drawn the head of a horse using nothing but a blue ballpoint pen. But it looked so real that Emily felt like she could reach out and touch it. On another was a sunset over a line of mountains, all drawn in pencil. Although there were no colors, Emily could easily imagine the yellows, reds, and purples in her mind.

She had just turned to a third drawing—a field of wildflowers—when she heard voices in the distance.

In the other hallway, she realized. *And it sounds like adults, too.*

She tossed the notebook back onto the shelf and closed the locker. Then she put the lock through the hole and shut it tight. A few seconds later, Principal Ellis came around the corner with Vice Principal Martin at his side.

With her heart pounding, Emily walked away and didn't look back.

Emily was standing in the yearbook room a little over eight hours later. And she felt like she was losing her mind.

It was an empty classroom on the second floor. Over the years, it had become a kind of all-purpose space. Students sometimes spent their detentions here. The drama club made their costumes here. Mrs. Stetser once tried holding her art class here. That ended when one of her students spilled a huge can of paint on the floor. During days of humid weather, you could still smell the paint.

Emily was at the whiteboard with a marker in hand. She looked every bit the boss that she truly was. Her staff sat in old classroom chairs behind her.

She pinched the bridge of her nose. A stress headache was coming on. "Listen, yearbook staff. We have one chance to do this right. We have to make our school look amazing. That's our *job*. The people in it, the building, the clubs, the awards. This is our Haddenport *legacy*."

The staff just looked at her, their faces unchanged. Where was their school spirit?

"Okay, Madeline, how are you coming with the timeline?"

Madeline Shaw had long dark hair and eyes that seemed just a bit too large for her face. She was writing a timeline of important things that had happened to their class over the last three years.

"I need to add a few more things to it," she said. She was sitting at one of the computers. "And then I'm done. Hey, should we include the time Oliver ran out for gym class without realizing he hadn't put his shorts on?"

"Definitely," Emily said. She looked over at Ms. Tanner to make sure this was okay. But Ms. Tanner never heard a word Madeline said. She was at the teacher's desk reading a magazine. She was young and pretty and not too thrilled that she'd been picked as this year's yearbook supervisor. Everyone here knew that Emily called the shots— not Ms. Tanner.

Emily turned to Madeline and mouthed the word "definitely" again. Madeline nodded with a smile and typed it in.

Turning back to the markerboard, Emily went to the next item on her list.

"Connor, how many more outside photos of the school do you need to take?"

Connor O'Leary was whip thin and had scraggly hair that reached almost to his shoulders. He was currently browsing through the pictures on his phone.

"I have enough now," he said without looking away. "There just isn't anything else interesting out there. Front of the school, side of the school, back of the school."

Emily put an X in the column called READY FOR PAGE LAYOUT.

"What about all four seasons? Did you—"

"Yes," Connor replied quickly. "Fall, winter, spring. And then I actually spent a day of my summer vacation at this awful place. Y'know, when I could have been out riding my skateboard. You're welcome."

"What incredible sacrifices you make for us," Emily said flatly.

"Right?" he said, her tone completely lost on him.

Back to the board again, Emily said, "Kaylee, do you and Charlotte have all the student photos now?"

Kaylee was at the computer next to Madeline. She was the tallest girl in class, and had a head of thick, autumn-red hair. The eyes behind her glasses were narrow and incredibly cheerful.

"Yes, we have them." There were at least a dozen of those pictures on the monitor. Emily checked her list. "And the bio stuff?"

"I have all the information now. I just need to type it under each picture. But it'll be done before the deadline, I promise."

"Excellent, Kay. Thanks."

She turned back to the whiteboard one more time, thinking how great Kaylee had been all along. Kaylee, Madeline, Matt, Danny, and yes, even Connor. They had all worked so hard on their yearbook assignments. Everything was coming in on time and looked terrific. It was the other three kids who made her nervous. Josh with his sports material. Hailey with her funny photos and captions. Chloe with her pictures of teachers and administrators.

Not only were they late, but Hailey hadn't been answering emails or text messages. She was barely posting on her socials. She never sat in the lunchroom and disappeared between classes. Emily was getting very fed up with it.

"Hey, Em," Kaylee called out, "could you take a look at this?"

Emily came up behind her and saw an enlarged photo of one student on the screen. It was Luke Travino, the smallest kid in their grade. He had light brown hair that was combed so perfectly it almost looked fake. And, as usual, he looked as frightened as a mouse.

Emily read the one line of text beneath the picture out loud—"'I live on Sycamore Lane with my parents.' Wow, that's it? That's all he gave us?"

Kaylee shrugged. "That's it."

"Did you ask him for more? I mean, everyone else wrote so much about themselves that we had to cut some of it."

Kaylee shook her head. "I did ask, and he said no. I got the impression he didn't even want to put *that*."

Emily shrugged. "Well, we can't make him give us more."

"No, I guess not." Kaylee chuckled. "He always was such a secretive kid, even when he was little, remember? Like he wanted to be such a mystery or something."

Emily shrugged. "I guess."

She turned to go back to the whiteboard, then stopped.

Always wanted to be a mystery … wait a second …

And right after that, the idea fell into place—

One of the old yearbooks—Sage Kimenski would have to be in there. She'd HAVE to be.

"Emily?" a voice behind her asked. "Are you okay?"

"Huh? Oh, yeah," she replied. "Fine." She nearly tripped over a chair in her rush. "I'll be back in a second. Keep working."

The old yearbooks were kept in a dusty corner of the library where no one ever went. Emily had noticed them before but never had any reason to touch them.

They were in order by year, she saw, starting as far back as 1964. She supposed her parents would be in a few of them. Probably the parents of some of her friends, too. But she didn't have time to check that out right now.

She found the one from the year Sage Kimenski had written on her notebook—2002. Pulling it from the others, she flipped noisily from one page to the next. Kimenski wasn't part of the sixth-grade class, nor the seventh. *So it was the eighth*, Emily thought, *the year she graduated.*

She fanned quickly through the remaining pages with her thumb. This created a little breeze that blew her hair around. When she reached the K section, her eyes widened. But when she finally reached Kimenski's spot, there was no feeling of excitement. Instead, it was pure shock from head to toe.

There *was* no picture for Sage Kimenski. In fact, there was no one named Sage at all.

"As if she never existed at all," Emily said softly.

Emily got home just before dinner and went straight to her room. Her mom had picked up sushi on the way back from work, but Emily said she'd eat hers later. It was rare for her to turn down sushi under any circumstances. What happened next was even more unusual—she decided her homework could wait, too. She had always been one of those kids who did their homework as soon as possible. Not today, though.

She closed her bedroom door and sat down at the computer. Then she got on Google and typed two things—SAGE KIMENSKI and HADDENPORT, NEW JERSEY.

Her mouth fell open in surprise when no

good results came back. There were plenty with two or three of those words, but none with all four.

"Wow, I thought Google could find *anything*."

She tried again, this time removing NEW JERSEY. Like before, not a single result came back that was useful. There was a car repair shop called Kimenski's Auto Center. And a candy shop called Sage's Kandies in Breston Heights. But nothing on the ghost-like Sage Kimenski.

Like she never existed in the first place … she thought again.

"Which is impossible," Emily said to the screen. "If she never existed, there wouldn't be all that mystery surrounding her locker. She wouldn't've had a locker in the *first* place."

Plus there was the notebook, she reminded herself. That was something she'd seen with her own eyes and touched with her own hands. There was writing on it, too. Writing that was made by a real person using a real pen.

She tried a new search—just SAGE KIMENSKI, nothing else. That produced quite a few results. The problem was that none of those people lived anywhere near Haddenport. It didn't surprise Emily that there were others in the world with that name. She had googled her own name once and found literally hundreds of other Emily Turners. (This had mostly shocked her. But it also depressed her a little bit for reasons she couldn't quite understand.)

So the fact that there were other Sage Kimenskis wasn't a big deal. But as Emily scrolled through the list, she didn't see any of the right age. She had already done the math on this. For one of those people to be the Sage Kimenski who once had Locker 24, she would have to be in her early thirties now. None were anywhere near that.

Emily hated putting effort into something and getting nothing in return. Wasted energy, wasted time … those things drove her nuts. But they also made her more determined. She was a really good Googler. Friends came to her all the time for help with this. She had a weird knack for finding almost anything.

As she set her hands on the keyboard once more, her mind went into Google-search hyperdrive—

SAGE KIMENSKI HADDENPORT MIDDLE SCHOOL

Nothing.

SAGE KIMENSKI HADDENPORT

Nothing.

SAGE KIMENSKI HADDENPORT ARTIST

Nothing.

SAGE KIMENSKI ARTIST NEW JERSEY

Nothing.

SAGE KIMENSKI ARTIST

Nothing.

Emily's jaw tightened as the frustration grew. "No! This is just not possible! There has to be *SOME* record of her!"

SAGE KIMENSKI ARTIST FROM THE TOWN OF HADDENPORT

Nothing.

SAGE KIMENSKI PROFESSIONAL ARTIST UNITED STATES

Nothing.

Emily whisper-screamed so no one would hear her downstairs. Then, more as a joke than anything else, she typed in—

SAGE KIMENSKI LOCKER 24

And that's when something came up.

It was just one result, right at the top. But as soon as she saw it, she knew why she'd been having so much trouble. The girl's name wasn't really Sage—it was Adriana.

Emily clicked on the link. It brought her to a blog for people who lived in Haddenport. The username of the person who started the thread was MissMarple. And the post was from 2014—

Hey, does anyone remember that girl Adriana from the middle school? The weird one who never talked to anybody?

The only response came from someone with the screen name DoItAgainIn2010—

Yeah, I do. Adriana Kimenski. Black hair, weird clothes. She was the one who was really good at art, right?

MissMarple: That's right. Whatever happened to her? Do you know?

DoItAgainIn2010: I have no idea. Wasn't she in high school with us? Or did she move?

MissMarple: I don't remember. That's the weird thing—she just sort of faded away like a ghost. And didn't she have that locker that's still closed? Locker 24?

DoItAgainIn2010: I think so, yeah. I heard no one's allowed to go near it.

MissMarple: I heard that, too. Someone was talking about it in the supermarket today. That's what made me think of her. So, no idea what happened to her?

DoItAgainIn2010: No idea.

And that's where the thread ended.

Emily smiled. "So it's Adriana Kimenski, not Sage. Got it …"

She started a fresh Google search with **ADRIANA KIMENSKI** and **HADDENPORT.** This time four results immediately came up containing all those keywords. They all connected to a single newspaper article. That seemed strange enough considering how hard Adriana had clearly worked to keep herself in the shadows. But what was even more bizarre was that it was from a newspaper in Kansas.

That's in the middle of the country, Emily thought. *At least a thousand miles from here.*

As soon as the article appeared on the screen, her eyes bulged. It wasn't just any article— it was Adriana Kimenski's obituary.

Then she saw the date, and every inch of her body turned cold.

"Two days ago," she said hollowly. "She … died … two … days … ago."

The same day, Emily also realized, *that I first found her locker open.*

Emily usually slept like a champ. Work hard, sleep hard. But not that night. The fact that Adriana Kimenski had died the same day that the locker had opened itself was creepy enough. But *why*? And why was it opening only for *her*?

Adriana's obituary didn't say much. It only said she died suddenly at her home in Kansas. Few people had commented on her memorial site online. Donations could be sent to an organization that helped people with mental illness.

Emily was still wondering about this the next morning as she walked down the empty early morning hallway the next day. She tried her best not to look at the locker as she went past it. But her eyes seemed to shift in that direction on their own. The locker was closed, she saw with some relief. *Maybe it's giving me a day off. Like a little break or something. Wouldn't that be nice?*

She got to her own locker and went through the normal routine. Some stuff in, some stuff out. Now she was thinking about the yearbook disaster again. Well, it wasn't quite a disaster yet … but it was getting close. A few more days and she'd officially be in full-panic mode. That's when she'd have to wave the white flag and ask Ms. Tanner for help. There was nothing in the world she dreaded more. *I'd rather have a dentist remove one of my teeth with a butter knife. Help is for the weak.*

"Josh, Hailey, and Chloe …" she mumbled. "Once I have their stuff, I'll have everything." Then it was just a matter of laying out the last few pages. That would be done right on the computer.

And if worse came to worst, she could do it herself. If it meant she'd have to stay late a few days, then so be it. That's what she'd do.

She zipped her bag shut and closed her locker. Then she turned and saw that Locker 24 was open just a little.

Her shoulders drooped as the misery spread across her face.

"No, please," she said in child's pouty voice. "Not today."

Emily went over to Locker 24 as if it was Adriana herself.

"I really can't today. I *can't*."

The locker didn't respond in any way. Not

that she expected it to. She looked to both ends of the hallway to see if anyone was around. But just like every other time, she was alone.

"Look," she continued. "I'm sorry you died, I really am. But what do you want from *me?* I didn't know you. I wasn't even alive when you went here! I don't know what you *want!*"

For a few seconds, nothing happened. Then, just as Emily was about to walk away, the door began to open further. It was the strangest thing she'd ever seen. The door moved by itself. A little groan sounded from its hinges. When it was about halfway open, it stopped.

"Umm … so what?" Emily said with a shrug. "I'm not seeing anything I didn't see yesterday. So what?"

Nothing else happened. The locker seemed to be done for the moment.

"Okay, I really don't know what I'm

supposed to do here. What do you want? For me to look at *this* again?"

She took the notebook from the shelf and thumbed through it. The artwork she saw yesterday, then more artwork. Some birds in the sky. A sunny seashore with palm trees. A snake coiled around a high tree branch.

"The math book, then? Am I supposed to check that out?"

She took it down and fanned through it. There was nothing unusual inside. No folded-up notes between the pages. No map to something buried in the woods. Just a lot of—

"—equations and formulas. Big deal."

She put that back, too.

"Okay, well, I've got a million things to do today, so I'm going now." She started closing the door. "It's been real, but I'll catch you lat—"

That's when she saw the ticket stub. Or at

least the edge of it, sticking out of the pocket of Adriana's windbreaker.

Wait, was that there last time?

She took a step back. Then, in her mind, she replayed the first time she looked inside. She went through the jacket's pockets then. The gum wrapper, the coins, the old pen …

There's no way I didn't see a ticket stub, she thought. *I'm certain of it.*

She reached down and took it out.

It was about the size and shape of a business card. Along one edge were the words STARLIGHT MOVIE CINEPLEX. That was the theater in Kings Valley, which was next to Haddenport. The name of the movie was printed in the center—*The Time Trap*.

"Never heard of it," she said. "Okay, so why is this impor—"

But the locker was closed again, the lock firmly back in place.

Emily left school very late that day. She was even more tired than usual. Two tests plus wind sprints in gym. And another big session in the yearbook room.

"We've got one day left before the deadline," she was saying into her phone as she walked outside. There weren't too many kids left. Just a few hanging around on the sidewalk or the grass.

"I know it's tomorrow," her mom said from the other end of the call. "You've been giving me a daily countdown for the last two weeks."

"Sorry."

Her mom laughed. "That's okay, sweetheart,

I'm just teasing. Did you get the rest of the material from everybody?"

"Almost. Josh and Chloe came through with their stuff today, *finally*. Honestly, Josh is never going to be a professional writer. But his photos are okay. And he's like a middle school celebrity so people will like them."

"That's excellent. So who's still holding you up?"

Emily closed her eyes and shook her head. "Now it's just Hailey. The funny pictures and captions."

"Can you live without those if you had to?"

Emily reached the sidewalk and turned left. "I *could*, yeah. But I'd prefer not to. The yearbook will be too serious without them. And who wants a serious yearbook? Come on, we're in *eighth grade!*"

"I get it," her mom replied. "When I was

going to your school, our class did some pretty ridiculous stuff. I remember one time our principal, Mr. Shadiack, made this deal with the kids. If we each read ten books in ten weeks, he'd spend the following week on the roof."

"Seriously?"

"Seriously. So we all read our books, even the kids who didn't like reading. We wanted to see if he'd really do it. And he did. He sat up there doing his work for a whole week."

"How'd they get the desk up there?"

"It wasn't the same one from his office. It was a big table and a chair they had lying around. And they used a set of stairs in the room where the furnace was. Y'know, stairs that the kids weren't allowed to go near."

"Wow." Emily was nodding now. "That *is* pretty cool."

"The town newspaper wrote an article about

it. And we used some of their pictures in our own yearbook."

Her mom's mention of the town newspaper made her think about Bryce. From there she thought about her conversation with him about Locker 24. Then she thought again about Adriana. And that led her to an amazing realization …

Wait, wasn't my mom going to school around the same time as her?

"—you still there, Em?"

Emily came out of her thoughts and back into the present.

"Huh? Oh, yeah. Sorry. Hey, can I ask you something?"

"About what?"

"About one of the students that you used to—"

But the words died away as she turned the corner and saw Hailey in the school's parking lot.

She was standing by a nice sports car, talking to the driver. There was someone sitting in the passenger seat as well.

"Oh, hang on," she said. "I just spotted Hailey. I'm going to see if I can catch her."

Hailey and the driver noticed Emily at the same time. Then the car pulled away.

"Hey!" Hailey said with a smile.

"Hey. I'm sorry, I didn't mean to interrupt you."

"Oh no, it's fine."

"Was that Brady and his brother?" Emily asked. Brady Clarke was in their grade, and his older brother, Darren, was a senior in high school. They were both part of the "rich club" with Josh and the others. Their dad was an executive in a bank or something. Played tennis with the middle school principal.

"Yeah," Hailey said.

"I didn't know you hung out with any of those guys," Emily said. Hailey was a bit of a loner in school. A little awkward. A bit shy. Different from the rich kid crew in more ways than just her parents' bank account. She was the kind of person who had more friends online than in person.

Hailey shrugged. "I guess they can be nice when they want to be."

Weird … Emily thought.

Hailey looked down at her worn sneakers, covered in Sharpie doodles. "So, I'm guessing you want to ask about the pictures for the yearbook?"

Emily snapped back to the task at hand.

"Yeah, tomorrow's the last day. After that, we won't be able to use them. And I'd really like to have yours. Your pictures, and the things you write when you post them online, are always *so* funny. Why haven't you posted much lately?"

Hailey's face reddened when she heard this. It was like she was embarrassed by it or something.

"That's so nice of you to say," Hailey said. "I didn't think people appreciated them."

"It's true," Emily said, making sure to meet Hailey's eyes. "The yearbook won't be the same without them! So can you stop by the yearbook room tomorrow after classes?"

"No problem."

"Okay, great. Thanks, Hail."

"Sure," Hailey said, and walked away, looking around her as if someone might be watching.

Emily's mom was making dinner when she got home that day. "You're home early," her mom said.

Emily threw her heavy bookbag on a kitchen chair. "Yeah, I thought we could, like, talk or something."

Emily's mom looked surprised. Emily didn't normally come home so soon, and she almost never spent time with her mom anymore. She was far too busy. But this was important.

"Talk about what?"

"Well," said Emily. "I was wondering if you know anything about Adriana Kimenski."

Emily's mom insisted that they go for a walk around the neighborhood. It was like she didn't want to say anything in the house.

"Okay," her mom began as soon as they got to the sidewalk. "So why are you asking about Adriana Kimenski?"

Emily told her what had happened over the last few days. It all sounded so *weird*, but she told the truth and left out nothing. Her mom seemed to take it all in. She knew her daughter would never lie about something like this. Emily felt relief after she'd told her.

"So yeah," Emily finished. "It's all really creepy. But I don't get the impression Adriana's ghost—or whatever it is—wants to hurt me. I just wish I knew what she did want. Then I realized you went to school around the same time as her. So maybe you could help or something. Maybe you know something about her that I can't find out."

They turned another corner and headed down Oakley Avenue.

"Okay," her mom said, nodding. "Yeah, I went to school with her. We were the same age and everything. She came here in the fourth grade, so she wasn't here long. And she was barely here when she *was* here."

"Huh? What does that mean?"

"She was one of those kids who sort of lived along the edge of our lives. Not in the middle of it like everyone else, y'know? You'd notice her once in awhile, but that was about it. It's like she was a ghost. And when she finally moved away, I don't think anyone realized for awhile."

"So she *did* move away."

"Yes, over the summer after we graduated eighth grade. She was gone before we all went to the high school."

"Do you know why she went by the name Sage?"

"Oh, she used different names all the time. That was just one of them."

"Huh?"

"Yeah. I remember she was Raven for a while. Then she wanted everyone to call her Grey."

Emily laughed a little. "That's a bit odd."

"Well, she *hated* the name 'Adriana.' I think it was her grandmother's name or something. And she was always trying to be artsy. Trying on new identities was part of it. Truthfully, most kids thought she was just a freak."

Emily frowned. "How come she and her family moved away?"

Emily's mom didn't say anything for a few

moments. She looked like she was thinking about her answer very carefully.

Her mom took a deep breath. "I sort of remember something happening to her. She met some of the other kids from school at the mall. Some real jerks. It was all a setup. I don't know what happened, exactly, but I heard she was never the same after that."

"Why did they target her?"

"Because she was kind of … odd."

"Odd? In what way?"

They came to Oakley Park, a small playground tucked in a grove of cedar trees. Her mom went and sat on one of the swings. Emily took the one next to her.

"Adriana really was a very nice person," her mom continued. "But there were things about her that were different. Things that set her apart from everyone else. She dressed in weird clothes. Really bright colors or all black. Thrift-store finds. Weird combinations. Her hair and makeup were always *out there*, too."

Emily made a face that mixed equal parts anger and confusion. "So what's wrong with that? We have tons of kids who fit that description in my school!"

"And how do people treat them?" her mom asked. Emily didn't have an answer—she'd never really noticed. Haddenport was the best school, the best people. There definitely weren't any *bullies* there. Bullies were something you saw on TV.

"Fine," Emily said, almost believing herself.

Her mom shook her head. "Well, when I was your age, people weren't so fine with different people. And no one who ran the school was very understanding."

"What do you mean?"

Her mom lowered her head in a way that

made her seem embarrassed.

"There are always going to be bullies in schools. Those types who want to be mean to anyone who isn't like them. And Adriana was different in so many ways. None of it bothered *me*, but it certainly bothered some kids."

"Like who—"

" … and teachers … and guidance counselors … and administrators."

"Whoa, what?"

"Adults can be bullies, too," said Emily's mom. "The kids said mean things to her or threw things at her. Their parents didn't want their kids being friends with her. And the people who worked at the school could be nasty to her, too. I remember one guy, a history teacher, who said things when he passed her in the hall. One I remember was 'Where do you buy your clothes, Adriana? From the mall on Mars?' Another was, 'Is that really how you wanted to wear your hair today? Or did a crow get stuck in it?'"

Emily was stunned. "If a teacher said something like that to a student now …"

"I know, he'd be looking for a new job in about two minutes," said her mom. "Anyway, Adriana kept taking all this abuse. Until one day something truly awful happened. And the kids who did it—the popular crowd—they weren't punished by the school because they were too well-connected. That's why no one wants to talk about her. And why no one's allowed near her locker. Her parents threatened to file a lawsuit against the school. There was supposed to be an investigation by the police and everything. Some of the stuff in her locker was going to be used in the case. But my guess is that the principal at the time was well-connected too. The case fizzled before anyone even opened her locker. Even after Adriana and her family moved away, the school refused to empty that locker. It might look like they were trying to destroy evidence. So it was never touched after that. No one spoke about Adriana again."

Emily was shaking her head. "Wow … just, wow."

"Yeah, tell me about it. You know how talented Adriana was, right?"

"Amazingly."

"Think about how much she could've done with that talent," said Emily's mom. "At my last school reunion someone told me that they'd kept in touch with Adriana. But that Adriana never made art again. After what happened, everything in her life started sliding downward. Remember, Em, things like this can affect us for the rest of our lives if we don't have the right support."

Emily thought sadly about all those incredible drawings she'd seen in that notebook.

Lots of people were creative and all that. But Adriana was on another level altogether. She could have been something great.

Her mom stopped, then hung her head. "Truthfully, I've thought about her a lot. I thought about how it all could've been avoided if she felt she had someone to turn to. How none of us stepped up."

Emily looked around at her neighborhood. One block away was her school, the one she rushed to every day. The one she wanted to paint in the best light possible through the yearbook. "Maybe things aren't as perfect here as I thought," she said.

A long silence hung between them. Then Emily said, "Okay, so now I know all the details. But I still don't know why Adriana pulled me into this."

"Whatever the reason, she thinks you're the right person."

Emily shook her head. "I don't know about that either, Mom."

"Why do you say that? You're one of the best kids I know."

"I don't know …" Emily looked off into the distance. For just a moment, it seemed like she might cry. "Y'know, I *have* seen kids get bullied before. Yeah, maybe not as often as when you were my age. But it still happens. You see a mean comment on social media and scroll past it. You see a kid get tripped in the hallway and step around."

"It's always going to happen," her mom reminded her. "Always. But as long as you're not the one doing it, then you—"

"No, Mom, don't say it. Don't say, 'then you're not to blame.' Okay, maybe I'm not actually doing the bullying myself. But that doesn't mean I'm totally *blameless.* I still saw it. I still heard about it. And I did nothing. *Nothing.*"

Her mom reached over and stroked her hair. "Yeah, I know all about that. Because I was the same way with Adriana."

"And now I feel like she wants me to help her," Emily said. "Okay, fine. I'm ready to do that. But *how*? Does she want me to do something with her artwork? Or have Bryce write an article about what really happened to her?"

"I don't know. I guess you'll find out in time. But can you do me one favor, Em?"

"What's that?"

"When you do figure it out, remember that I'm here to help, too. So is your dad. Maybe Adriana believed she was alone, but you're not. And for that matter, neither is she. Not anymore."

Adriana's locker wasn't open the next day. Not when Emily arrived early in the morning. Not when she walked past it on her way to lunch. And not when the bell rang after the last class. Her mind was on just one thing at that point anyway—*the deadline.* She had until five o'clock.

Minutes after she got to the yearbook room, she was sitting at one of the computers. The other kids—Kaylee, Madeline, Connor, Josh—were standing around, watching. There wasn't much left for them to do except give Emily emotional support.

She looked up at the clock every few minutes. When it reached 4:30, she said, "No sign of Hailey?"

Josh opened the door and looked around. "Nope." He smirked. "And by the way, I've got some better things to do, so …" He smiled that winning grin and Emily let him go.

Emily shook her head. "She promised she'd have everything ready. She *promised*."

"She wasn't in math class today," Madeline said.

"She wasn't in gym, either," Connor added.

Emily let out a long, weary sigh. "She picked a really bad day to be sick or whatever."

"Do you want me to call her?" Kaylee asked, reaching to her back pocket. "Y'know, as a last-shot kind of thing?"

Emily thought for a moment, then said, "No, I'll do it. And I'll try my best to be nice."

She put the call on speaker. It rang several times before going to voicemail. So she sent a text using all capital letters and quite a few exclamation points. That, too, received no response. She went onto Hailey's social media. Her last story was about some movie that just came out.

Emily returned to the computer.

"What happened?" Kaylee asked.

"She's not answering," Emily replied. "So, I guess we're going to have to—"

Then her brain connected the dots. The movie.

She went to see a movie.

From there, Emily remembered what Hailey had said in the parking lot after Brady and his older brother Darren drove off in such a hurry.

I guess they can be nice when they want to be.

Emily reached in her pocket and pulled out the movie ticket she found in Adriana's locker. She looked at the movie title one more time—*The*

Time Trap.

"You can't be serious," she mumbled. She turned back to the computer, went to Google, and typed it in. What came up next chilled her to her bones.

This isn't a movie from Adriana's time. It's a new movie that's playing right now. The one from Hailey's story. In fact, it's playing tonight.

And in that moment, everything became clear. The locker. The ticket stub. *Why Hailey turned and walked away from me in the hallway the other day. It wasn't me she was running from.*

"No, no, no …" she said nervously before tearing out of the room.

Kaylee called after her, "But, Emily—the yearbook!"

"The Starlight Cineplex," Emily said fifteen minutes later. She was leaning forward from the back seat of her parents' car.

"You're sure?" her dad asked from behind the wheel. He looked every bit the overworked accountant that he was—hair short and neat, steel-rimmed glasses.

"Yes," Emily replied. *At least as sure as I can be.*

"And *how* do you know this?"

"We'll explain later," her mom said from the front passenger seat. "It's a long story."

Emily's dad gave her a puzzled look. Then Emily tapped him on the shoulder.

"Pay attention, Dad. And go faster!"

"Ems, if I go any faster, I won't be driving the car, I'll be flying it."

He made another right turn, and the strip mall with the theater came into view. There was a supermarket all the way to the left called Angelo's. Then a beauty salon, a Dairy Queen, and a hardware store. And finally, on the right, was the Starlight.

As her dad entered the parking lot, her mom scanned the crowd along the sidewalk. "I don't see Hailey anywhere," she said.

Emily checked her watch. "The movie's just about to start. She must be inside already!"

They parked in the closest spot they could find and ran inside. Emily's dad grumbled when he had to buy a ticket for each of them.

Just as they got near the doors that led to the theater, they saw her. She was wearing a beautiful black dress and standing next to Brady.

Emily came to a stop. "Wait a minute …
what?"

Her parents stopped, too, on either side of
her.

"Is that … Brady Clarke?" her mom asked.
His family had lived in their neighborhood Emily's
whole life.

Emily nodded. "Uh, yeah." The fact that he
was with Hailey was just too strange.

Hailey and Brady opened the double doors
and went inside.

"So that's all that's happening here?" Emily's
dad asked, sounding a little peeved. "Two kids are
going to see a movie together?"

Emily opened her mouth to say I *guess*
so. But then another door opened. It was for the
bathroom on the other side of the hallway. Three
boys came out, giggling like little children. Emily

recognized them right away. One was Darren, Brady Clarke's older brother. Then there was Max Gad. And then there was Josh. What caught her attention most of all, however, was the thing she saw Josh slip into his jacket pocket.

"*Hey,*" she heard herself say with quite a bit of anger. The boys halted like they'd been hit by a stun gun. Then the smiles disappeared from their faces.

"Oh, hey Emily," Josh said with that winning grin. "What are you do—"

"You ran out of the yearbook meeting," she said. "Whatcha got in your pocket there?"

An embarrassed redness spread over his face.

"Nothing," Josh said.

"Don't lie to me," Emily said. She was surprised by how angry she sounded. "Take them out, right now."

The three boys looked at each other. Then Darren and Max looked at Josh for his answer.

"You have no idea how much you'll hurt her," Emily said.

There was another long moment of uncomfortable silence. Emily knew that her social standing—athlete, straight-A, well-liked—could make them listen. She was risking all of that. But it didn't matter. Only Hailey mattered.

"You serious?" Josh asked.

"Serious," said Emily.

The boys reached into their pockets and took out several balloons loaded with water.

After they were thrown away, Darren said sheepishly, "We just thought it would be funny."

"That's the problem with bullies," Emily replied. "You only think about how it feels for *you*. It's *not* funny."

She burned them with her eyes for a few more seconds. Until Josh looked down at his feet. Then she went into the theater to get Hailey.

"The printing company is giving us another few days," Emily said as she opened the front door of the school the following Monday. "Turns out, all I had to do was ask."

"Oh, that's fantastic," her mom replied through the earbud. "You deserve the extra time. Plus, asking for what you need isn't a sign of weakness."

Emily rolled her eyes. But she knew her mom was right. It was okay to ask for help. It was okay to reach out to others. She knew that now. "Most importantly," Emily said, "the new yearbook is going to reflect the school as it really is. And that means less of a platform for kids like Josh—and more for talented kids like Hailey."

"She finally handed in her pictures?"

Emily nodded as she went past a row of trophy cases. "Those pictures and more. I'm giving her a whole spread. Her work is real. And it's *really* funny."

"That's great. I'm so happy for you."

Emily was happy, too. This yearbook was coming to a close. She'd been thinking about what she wanted to do next. She loved staying busy, but she was feeling a little like her phone when the battery got too low. *I need recharging,* she decided. And if there was one thing she'd learned in all this it was that she needed to stop and notice. She'd been in such a hurry that she didn't see Hailey being bullied or set up.

"So anyway, they were really teasing Hailey online, too?" her mom asked.

"Yeah. She told me it's been happening for a while. Josh and his friends had been leaving nasty comments on her socials. Whispering mean things to her in the hallway. That's why she stopped putting up those funny pictures with the great captions. And why she didn't want to put any in the yearbook, either. She was too embarrassed."

"And just like Adriana, she felt she had no one to go to for help," said Emily's mom. "You know, I called Hailey's mom after what happened. Let's just say, it doesn't seem like Hailey has much support at home either."

Emily bit her lip. "I can't imagine not having anyone to turn to." She felt so lucky to have her mom. "Plus, Josh's family practically runs this school. She didn't think the school would do anything."

"Ridiculous. *Are* they going to get into trouble?" her mom asked.

"I think they're getting a week's detention," Emily told her.

"They should be getting a lot more than that. The whole date thing with Brady was a setup from the beginning. Pretending he was her friend and everything. Horrible. They just wanted to humiliate her."

"They planned to livestream it for the whole eighth grade to see online. Well, if they do anything like that again, they'll all be suspended. That's what I heard."

Her mom let out a little grunt. "I guess that's something. Poor Hailey. Imagine if you hadn't been there to stop those boys."

Emily had been thinking about this a lot over the weekend. This was exactly why Adriana had reached out to her from beyond. The moment Adriana was set up for humiliation was also the moment her life started falling apart. It was like being in some weird house where every time you went into a room, the one behind you changed, making it impossible for you to get back to where you were. Adriana knew this was going to happen to Hailey and wanted to stop it.

"It was Adriana—not me," Emily said. "She's the real hero in all of this."

Emily went around the corner to the hallway with all the lockers. She stopped in her tracks. Mr. Hadermeyer was standing at Locker 24, taking out each item and setting it neatly in a cardboard box.

"Hey, Mr. H," Emily said, "what's going on?"

"I've got orders to pack up everything in here so it can be mailed out."

"Seriously?"

"Seriously."

"Let me guess—an address in Kansas?"

Mr. Hadermeyer stopped and looked at her

curiously. "Now how in the world would you know that?"

Emily shrugged. "I've heard some things."

The old man put his hands on his hips and let out a sigh. "Well, I've been told not to discuss this locker for the last twenty years. But I remember the girl who had it, and she was a *nice* girl. She really was. A little strange, maybe, but I've learned in my lifetime that strange is okay. She was a *good* kind of strange, y'know? So maybe it's okay for us to talk about this locker now. And maybe about the girl who had it, too."

Emily nodded. "Maybe it's time for it to be okay for people to talk about a lot of things they couldn't before," she said. "And then we can all learn from it and do better."

Mr. Hadermeyer nodded. "I think you're right, Emily," he replied. "I think you're exactly right." Then he went back to work.

Emily walked on to her own locker. "You heard all that, didn't you?" she said. She'd forgotten her mom was still on the call.

"I did," her mom replied through the earbud. "So what are you doing after school today? Yearbook? Chess club? Track? Taking up the banjo? Ruling the world?"

Emily laughed. She opened her locker and set her backpack on the floor like always. But before she had a chance to do anything else, she noticed something different. The heart sticker that had been on the inside of Adriana's locker door was now on hers. And the single word that was printed on it seemed more important than ever—

LOVE

Emily looked up and saw Hailey walking toward her, a small smile on her face. New purple streaks in her hair. "Actually," she told her mom, waving to Hailey. "I'll be home early for dinner. And I'm bringing a friend."

Want to Keep Reading?

Turn the page for a sneak peek at
another book in the series.

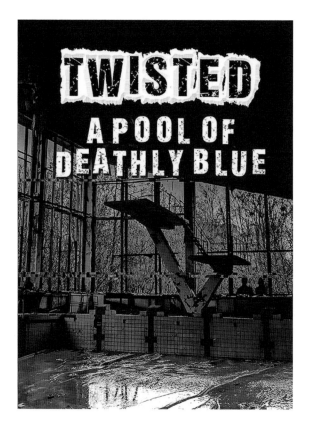

ISBN: 9781978595286

It seemed like a perfect morning. The sun had just started to rise. Birds were chirping and chittering in the trees. And the house where Mason and Madison Page lived stood as tall and proud as ever.

It was the nicest house on the block— probably the whole town. Mr. Page worked in the city in a fancy bank. Mason and Madison didn't know much more than that. But they did know he made tons of money. And because of that, they had this gigantic house.

One room had an enormous flat-screen TV and three rows of large, comfortable chairs. This was the family's personal movie theater. There was also a game room in the basement. It had another big TV screen, just for video games. And there was a soda machine that didn't need any money. You just pressed one of the plastic buttons, and out came an ice-cold bottle. Their parents had hoped buying them all these things would bring them together as a family. But Madison and Mason weren't much into family time at home. Even if they did have pinball machines and an air-hockey table.

And then there was the pool.

It was in the backyard, and it had a diving board and a slide. It also had a heater so the water felt bathtub-warm. There was a patio with a fire pit and an outdoor kitchen. Two guys from a cleaning service came twice a week to keep the pool spotless. Since there was no wind on this particular morning, the surface of the water remained perfectly still. It could have been a sheet of glass, reflecting a few sluggish clouds in an otherwise clear blue sky.

Then, just after a flock of sparrows passed overhead, it began to change. The color of the blue became lighter. Then darker. Then light again, then dark again. The water began to swirl and churn—first one way, then the other. Bubbles rose to the surface by the thousands. Waves formed, rolling from one end to the other. Water slapped against the sides, sloshing onto the walkway. More bubbles came up, millions now. They turned into a sudsy foam, filling the pool.

Just as quickly as all this had started, it settled down again. The foam broke apart. The waves declined in stages. The swirling vanished with one final spin. The water returned to its calm state. A sheet of glass again, reflecting the same collection of unhurried clouds. Only the shade of blue had changed. It was most unusual. A shade rarely seen in this world. A deathly shade.

And there was something at the bottom of

the pool now. Something that hadn't been there before.

A few minutes later, Madison Page came out the back door. She was like her twin brother in so many ways. Sandy blonde hair, green eyes, athletic build. They were thirteen. Mason had been born first, which meant he was about a minute older. And he never let Madison forget it.

She walked to the end of the patio and then froze. In the next yard, she could hear them—three kids around her age, playing volleyball, probably with their broken net. She turned as quietly as she could and began tiptoeing away.

The door swung open again, and Mason stepped out. He was dressed in a T-shirt, gym shorts, and brand-new sneakers. He walked like he was popular, which was true.

Madison waved to get his attention, then put a finger to her lips. "Shh—the Halleys are out there right now…"

Mason smiled. "Are they digging in the dirt for worms to eat?"

Madison giggled. "You're awful."

He looked over at the house where the Halleys lived and shook his head.

"Can you seriously imagine living there?"

"Not for a zillion bucks."

It had been a running joke with them for years. The last owners, an elderly couple named the Clarksons, let the place fall apart. The paint was peeling, the screens had rips and tears, and there were shingles missing from the roof. The grass was too high and the shrubs were all scraggly.

But now there were new owners, the Halleys. A dad, a mom, and three kids. Mason and Madison thought maybe they'd fix the place up. No such luck. It turned out the father had lost his job or something, and that was the only house the family could afford. So there it sat, still rotting away. Mr. Page would rant about it at dinner. *If they'd just put some effort in...*

Honey, you don't know what they might be dealing with, Mrs. Page would reply.

But Madison and Mason agreed with their dad. It was their own fault they lived that way.

The fact that the Halley house was right next to *their* house was...well, embarrassing. So when the Halley kids tried to make friends with them, that was embarrassing, too. Those kids had tried everything, including knocking on their front door and leaving notes in their mailbox. The oldest one, Zac, was in their class, and he asked them to hang out all the time. They never said yes, but he just kept asking, which drove them crazy.

He was really smart, too, which bothered the Page twins. So they made fun of him as much as possible. When he got one question wrong on a math test, they began referring to him as "Zac the Hack." A few weeks ago, he gave a presentation on the Chernobyl nuclear disaster—some explosion at a nuclear power plant in Ukraine back in the 1980s. Madison had rolled her eyes as Zac got choked up about radiation raining down on the nearby town of Pripyat. His voice had cracked as he said "widespread illness and even deaths." Mason made jokes about how the survivors probably glowed at night. Zac probably did too because he did the report.

"Just the thought of hanging out with them," Mason said, shuddering. "Ugh..."

They were off the grass now and on the walkway that went around the pool.

"You know what we should do?" he went on. "We should—hey, what's wrong?"

Madison had stopped and was standing on the pool's edge now, staring down.

"Come here for a sec," she said.

"Okay..."

She pointed into the pool.

"Do you see that?"

Mason looked closely. At first it was difficult to see anything. There was a light breeze now, drawing ripples on the water's surface. Then it died down, and the water became perfectly clear again.

"Is that what I think it is?" he asked.

Madison nodded. "The locket that Grandma gave me."

It sat there at the very bottom, heart-shaped and shining. The chain squiggled around it like a dead snake.

"But you never wear it when you're swimming," Mason said. "You never wear it at *all*."

"I know."

"So how'd it get down there?"

Madison shook her head.

"No idea."

"Seriously, how is that possible?" Madison wondered. "I keep it on my dresser all the time."

"No idea, Maddy-poo."

"Don't call me that, zitface."

"Sorry, Maddy-poo. I really don't know what to tell you. But I do know one thing for sure..."

"What's that?"

"You should *go get it*!" He pushed her from behind.

With her arms pinwheeling wildly, Madison let out a scream that seemed to echo from one end of the galaxy to the other. Then she hit the water's surface and went under. When she came back up, she looked as mad as a rabid dog.

"You *jerk*!" she said, splashing him hard. "I just bought this shirt!"

"Stinks to be you," he said, his smile bigger than ever.

"And you're lucky my phone wasn't in my pocket! Dad would *kill* you if you ruined that!"

"Considering how much time you waste on that thing, I'm surprised you didn't—hey! Wait! *NO*!!!"

But it was too late—Madison jumped up, grabbed his wrist, and yanked him down. He landed with a mighty splash.

The moment he came back to the surface—his hair in a dripping rug over his eyes—she was waiting with a big smile of her own.

"Stinks to be *you*!" she said, laughing.

"Oh yeah? Well, guess what—if I get to that locket first, it's *mine*!" Then he dove under.

"No *WAY*!!!" Madison screamed, before

doing the same.

She grabbed him by the leg to slow him down. He reached up and pushed her hand away. When she tried to swim past him, he clutched her arm. This became a slow-motion slap fight. With their lungs aching, they gave up the battle and began moving downward again. Mason—always the better swimmer—reached the locket first and snatched it up. Madison screamed something to him that was lost in the blue. Mason stuck his tongue out at her. Then he planted his foot on the bottom of the pool and launched himself upward.

When Madison broke the surface seconds later, she already had her hand out.

"Give it back," she said angrily. "Right now!"

But Mason wasn't hearing her. His mouth hung open as if on broken hinges. His eyes were wide. She easily grabbed the necklace from him and stuffed it in her pocket.

But then Madison saw it, too. It was impossible. Just *impossible*.

"Mason..." she said, her voice shaking. "Wh-where are we?"

He didn't reply.

"Mason?" she asked again. Still nothing. His face was pale.

They were still in a pool, but it wasn't *their* pool. This one was inside a huge room with white tiles all over the walls and ceiling. On one side, windows covered the length of the wall.

"Where are we?" Madison asked again.

"I don't know." Mason shook his head quickly. This, she knew, was how he acted when he was nervous. His words, his movements—

everything became faster.

He swam to the closest ladder. There were two concrete diving platforms nearby. They were both attached to the same V-shaped stand, one a few feet higher than the other.

Mason got out and went to the window-wall. Then he froze. Madison had never seen him so scared before. That scared her even more.

She got out and went to the window. She saw what Mason was looking at.

"Oh my god..."

It was a ghost town. There were some trees close by, scraggly and dead. Tall apartment buildings stood nearby, with broken windows and blotches of black mold where the paint had been. The road was crumbling, with weeds breaking through the blacktop.

"What *is* this?" Madison whispered.

"I don't...I don't know."

Mason lingered there for another moment, his eyes now zombie-dead. Then he started walking away.

"Where are you going?"

"Out there."

"What? *Why*?!"

When he didn't answer, she hurried to catch up, her heart pounding.

ABOUT THE AUTHOR

Wil Mara has been writing and publishing for the last 35 years. With more than 300 books to his credit, he has written fiction and nonfiction for both children and adults. He is the author of the Twisted series for middle grade readers, as well as two series of early chapter books—Izzy Jeen the Big-Mouth Queen and Logan Lewis: Kid from Planet 27. His work has earned him numerous awards, the most recent being the 2019 Literary Lion Award from the Library of Congress, and the 2020 Author of the Year Award from the New Jersey Association of School Librarians. You can find out more about his books at www.wilmara.com.

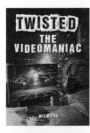

THE VIDEOMANIAC

HOUSE OF A MILLION ROOMS

THE TIME TRAP

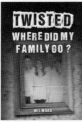

WHERE DID MY FAMILY GO?

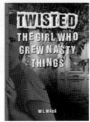

THE GIRL WHO GREW NASTY THINGS

A POOL OF DEATHLY BLUE

THE OTHER

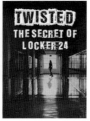

THE SECRET OF LOCKER 24

Check out more books at:

www.west44books.com

An imprint of Enslow Publishing

WEST 44 BOOKS™